Basketball Superstar LeBron James

by Jon M. Fishman

BUMBA BOOKS™

LERNER PUBLICATIONS ◆ MINNEAPOLIS

Note to Educators

Throughout this book, you'll find critical-thinking questions. These can be used to engage young readers in thinking critically about the topic and in using the text and photos to do so.

Lerner Publications Company
A division of Lerner Publishing Group, Inc.
241 First Avenue North
Minneapolis, MN 55401 USA

For reading levels and more information, look up this title at www.lernerbooks.com.

Main body text set in Helvetica Textbook Com Roman 23/49.
Typeface provided by Linotype AG.

Library of Congress Cataloging-in-Publication Data

Names: Fishman, Jon M, author.
Title: Basketball superstar Lebron James / by Jon M. Fishman.
Description: Minneapolis, MN : Lerner Publications, [2020] | Series: Bumba books. Sports superstars | Includes bibliographical references and index. | Audience: Age 4–7. | Audience: K to Grade 3.
Identifiers: LCCN 2018043340 (print) | LCCN 2018049922 (ebook) | ISBN 9781541557390 (eb pdf) | ISBN 9781541557376 (lb : alk. paper) | ISBN 9781541573628 (pbk)
Subjects: LCSH: James, LeBron—Juvenile literature. | Basketball players—United States—Biography—Juvenile literature. | African American basketball players—Biography—Juvenile literature.
Classification: LCC GV884.J36 (ebook) | LCC GV884.J36 F56 2020 (print) | DDC 796.323092 [B]—dc23

LC record available at https://lccn.loc.gov/2018043340

Manufactured in the United States of America
3-53337-45949-5/4/2022

Table of Contents

King James

LeBron James shoots.

Swish!

He is a basketball

superstar.

SAC
35
23
40
10

LeBron plays for the Los Angeles Lakers. He is one of the best players in the world.

How do people become good at sports?

9:23
22
TISSOT
BLAZERS
16
BLAZERS
27
NBA
League
Pass

adidas
IRISH
23

LeBron was a great player
in high school.
Basketball made him famous.

After high school, he joined the Cleveland Cavaliers. He helped the team win.

How can a player help a team win?

LeBron switched teams in 2010.

He joined the Miami Heat.

HEAT
6

2012 NBA
CHAMPIONS
ESPN

Miami was a good team.

LeBron helped them

become champions two

years in a row.

Then LeBron went back to Cleveland.

Cleveland soon became champions too!

SPALDING
23

UCLA Health
LOS ANGELES LAKERS
Health
wish
LAKERS

LeBron switched teams again.

This time, he joined Los Angeles.

LeBron helped Los Angeles become champions! Fans love to watch him play hard for his team.

wish
LAKERS
23
8

Basketball Gear

Picture Glossary

champions

winners of the top prize

famous

known by many people

joined

became part of something

shoots

throws the ball at the basket

Read More

Flynn, Brendan. *Basketball Time!* Minneapolis: Lerner Publications, 2017.

Rebman, Nick. *Basketball.* Lake Elmo, MN: Focus Readers, 2019.

Schuh, Mari. *Basketball.* Mankato, MN: Amicus, 2018.

Index

Photo Credits

Image credits: Amy Salveson/Independent Picture Service (basketball icons throughout); Kevork Djansezian/Getty Images, pp. 5, 23 (bottom right); Steve Dykes/Getty Images, pp. 6–7, 21; Steve Grayson/WireImage/Getty Images, pp. 8, 23 (top right); Andrew Weber/Icon Sportswire/Getty Images, pp. 10–11; Marc Serota/Getty Images, p. 13; DON EMMERT/AFP/Getty Images, pp. 14, 23 (top left); BECK DIEFENBACH/AFP/Getty Images, p. 17; FREDERIC J. BROWN/AFP/Getty Images, pp. 18, 23 (bottom left); Mr.nutnuchit Phutsawagung/EyeEm/Getty Images, p. 22 (basketball); Zovteva/Shutterstock.com, p. 22 (jersey); dnaveh/iStock/Getty Images, p. 22 (shoes); NAKphotos/iStock/Getty Images, p. 22 (shorts).

Cover: Steve Dykes/Getty Images.